Whispers of the Banyan Tree

by Belinda Chavremootoo

Dedication

For those who remember what was never written down.

And for those who listen when the land speaks.

About the Author

Belinda writes stories for grown-ups and kids—cozy mysteries with garden gates and clever cats, magical adventures where shy voices find their roar, and now, quiet mysteries where history murmurs through banyan leaves.

Her fiction often wanders between folklore and family, justice and memory—grounded in vivid places and layered characters. *Whispers of the Banyan Tree* is her first literary mystery, and the beginning of a new journey into stories shaped by roots and reckoning.

When she's not writing, she's usually in her garden, dreaming up characters between the tomatoes and thyme, while her two cats supervise with serious faces and zero chill.

Epigraph

"There was a child buried under the banyan, they say. Not for punishment. Not for sacrifice. For silence."

— Field note, Cultural Archives of Île de Céleste (unverified)

Five roots buried, five coins paid.

One boy waits, his name unmade.

He does not sleep. He does not weep.

The land will wake what we try to keep.

— fragment of a lullaby, origin unknown

Table of Contents

Prologue

The island greeted her with silence.

Not the kind tourists wrote about—the kind laced with waves and birdsong and wind in the palms—but the other kind. The kind that seeped into the soil and waited.

Alisha Desai stepped off the ferry before dawn, the air thick with salt and secrets. Fog clung to the harbour like it belonged there, refusing to lift. Her boots hit the dock with the quiet thud of someone returning somewhere they never meant to come back to.

Île de Céleste hadn't changed. Not really. The sugarcane still bowed in the same places. The same chipped statue of St.

Brigitte leaned into the sea breeze. The same graffiti— *"Land isn't empty just because you don't hear it scream"*—faded near the port warehouse.

She tugged her coat tighter.

A woman sold fried breadfruit from a rusted cart. A dog watched her pass like it recognized her soul. No welcome party. No banners. No homecoming.

Just... memory.

She pulled out a folded envelope from her bag. Her grandfather's handwriting still clear, even after eight years:

"If you return, listen to the land. She doesn't forget."

She hadn't come back for ghosts. But they were already lining up.

Her taxi was late, so she walked to the edge of the old botanical garden—what was left of it. The banyan trees had spread since her childhood, roots thick as limbs, limbs like arms. One root curved like a bench, and she sat, remembering.

It was here that Rajiv Desai once told her the story of the "boy who fed the tree."

She hadn't believed it. Not really.

But now, the root beneath her vibrated slightly.

Like a memory, waking.

A voice behind her said, "If you're sitting under that one, you either trust the island... or you don't know her yet."

She turned.

He looked like he'd slept in a library: oversized button-down, messy curls, eyes like he'd forgotten the difference between dreams and facts.

Noah Gopaul.

He offered her a half-smile and a folded pamphlet. *"The Ghost Trees of Belle Forêt: A Cultural Folklore Walking Tour."*

"I'm Noah," he said. "Archivist. Tour guide. Occasional buzzkill."

She raised an eyebrow. "I'm not here for a tour."

"No one ever is," he said, then nodded toward the roots. "That one's Bastian's tree. Or so they say."

She blinked.

"Who?"

But he was already walking away.

The jeep pulled up minutes later. A young constable waved her over, oblivious to the crackling moment.

Her phone buzzed.

Body confirmed. Belle Forêt. Courbet estate. Chief wants you on it. Now.

She looked once more at the tree, then stepped into the vehicle.

As they drove off, a breeze slipped through the branches.

The banyan whispered.

Chapter 1

The banyan tree had grown heavier over the years.

Its roots twisted like sleeping serpents through the courtyard stones, dipping into the bones of a land Jean-Michel Courbet had never fully claimed—though he'd bought it, sold it, rezoned it, and named a cocktail after it.

He took a sip of that very drink now— *Le Crépuscule*—rum, mango, lime, and a sliver of pickled tamarind. It burned slightly; in a way he liked. Below him, lanterns flickered across the garden. Foreign investors laughed too loud. Island music drifted upward, curated to feel authentic without offending sensibilities.

His estate—La Maison Marée—was dressed to impress.

But his eyes kept drifting to the tree.

The banyan stood at the edge of the lawn, where the manicured garden gave way to wild cane and salt air. Someone had strung fairy lights through its upper limbs. Festive. Decorative.

He hated it.

"You don't dress up a god," he muttered.

"Talking to trees now?" Simone stepped onto the balcony in silver silk, her voice soft, her disapproval sharp.

She followed his gaze. "You should be happy. Everyone's enchanted."

"I told them not to light the tree."

"It's a tree, Jean-Michel."

He didn't answer.

He couldn't explain the weight in his chest. The old stories he'd dismissed his whole life had started whispering again. Ever since they broke ground near the grove. Ever since the dreams.

Simone watched him. "Are you nervous?"

"Of course not."

"Then why are your hands shaking?"

He looked down.

They were. He laughed—short and brittle—and turned away. "Too much rum."

But even as he descended the steps into the party, he felt the banyan watching him.

Not just watching.

Waiting.

* * *

Simone watched him as he disappeared into the party crowd. Music swelled, glasses clinked, and the banyan faded behind him—for now.

But it never faded for long.

Later, after the toast and the speeches, after the fireworks bloomed and died above the sea, Courbet slipped away. Too many smiles. Too much noise.

He wandered the edge of the garden, toward the banyan.

The lights had gone out around it. Or been extinguished.

He approached slowly. The air was still. No frogs. No wind.

The scent of something—salt, copper, and something older.

He reached into his pocket. The silver coin was there. He kept it always now, ever since he found it during excavation. It bore no nation's mark, only a bird etched in crude lines. He didn't know why he carried it.

A sound—like breath, not wind.

He turned.

There was no one.

Then he felt it—just beneath the ear, a sharp prick, like a mosquito bite.

He touched the spot. Wet.

Courbet dropped his glass. It shattered, unheard.

The world blurred. His knees buckled.

The last thing he saw was the banyan's roots, open like arms.

Waiting.

Chapter 2

The sea was the same.

That was the first thing Alisha Desai noticed as the car wound along the coast road. After eight years away, the colours of Île de Céleste still stunned her—the cobalt sky, the jade hills, the sudden bursts of flame tree red along the sugarcane fields. But the sea—she remembered that best. As a girl, she had believed it whispered secrets. Now, older and trained in forensic logic, she suspected it still did.

Her phone buzzed. A message from HQ.

Body confirmed. Belle Forêt. Courbet estate. Chief wants you on it. Now.

She stared at the screen for a moment, then slipped the phone back into her coat pocket. No "welcome back," no briefing, just the weight of an island secret waiting to be exhumed.

She leaned back in the passenger seat of the police jeep. The driver, a junior constable named Davide, was silent—too silent for island standards. She could feel his discomfort like humidity.

"You've lived here your whole life?" she asked.

He nodded. "Yes, Inspector."

"Then you know the Courbet estate?"

Another nod. "Everyone knows it." A pause. "They say it's cursed. That tree especially."

Alisha raised an eyebrow. "That tree?"

"Big banyan. People disappear near it. Since plantation times." He hesitated. "You're not like the last inspector."

"No," she said, half smiling. "He played golf and wore linen suits. I solve murders."

He chuckled nervously, not sure if he was being tested.

***

They arrived just after sunset. Blue lights cut across the manicured lawn. The estate's white façade glowed faintly under lanterns, but the air had gone still. Party guests were clustered in murmuring groups, some weeping, some simply staring toward the banyan tree that loomed beyond the garden wall.

Alisha stepped out. The ground felt oddly soft beneath her boots.

A man in a worn leather jacket approached, mid-40s, Creole, wiry and watchful, with the steady presence of someone who'd seen every kind of mess and still made it home for dinner.

"Sergeant Emmanuel Roux. You can call me Manu," he said, extending a hand.

Alisha had read his file—fifteen years on the force, born in Belle Forêt, decorated once for defusing a hostage crisis and nearly fired twice for punching a corrupt superior. A man who knew this island's underbelly better than its beaches.

She shook his hand firmly. "Inspector Desai. You've got a murder?"

He grinned faintly. "I heard you were coming. Some people hoped it was a rumour."

He led her toward the edge of the party lawn. "Jean-Michel Courbet. Local royalty. Dead under that tree." He gestured to the banyan, now cordoned off by yellow tape. "No sign of a struggle. Just collapsed. We've sealed the scene."

Alisha approached the body. Courbet lay on his side in the grass, eyes wide, a shattered glass near his hand. His face was flushed, lips tinged slightly blue.

"He does not look surprised," she murmured.

Manu nodded. "Almost like he saw it coming too late."

A quiet voice spoke from behind them. "It wasn't natural."

Alisha turned, unsurprised.

Emerging from the shadows of the banyan tree came a familiar figure—elbows, curls, oversized messenger bag, and the same offbeat calm he'd had earlier that morning.

"You again," she said, arching a brow.

Noah Gopaul—historian, folklorist, and self-proclaimed "cultural archivist"—tilted his head. "You're early. Most people don't get haunted twice in one day."

Manu blinked. "Wait. You two know each other?"

"We met near the botanical ruins," Noah replied. "She sat under Bastian's root."

"I didn't know it had a name," Alisha muttered.

"It didn't, until someone remembered."

Half-French, half-Indian, and wholly obsessed with the island's past, he spoke with the speed of a man who thought in parentheses.

"This tree," he began without greeting, "has been in oral records since at least the 1700s. There's a story—several actually—about a boy who was buried here alive. He's supposed to protect the grove. People used to leave coins in the roots."

Manu gave Alisha a look. "This is Noah. He knows too much, talks too much, but he's usually right."

Noah adjusted his glasses. "That's the nicest thing you've ever said to me."

Manu rolled his eyes. "Noah's our in-house walking encyclopaedia. You'll get used to him."

"I'm not superstitious," Noah said. "But the story's always the same. A man who dishonours the grove dies without a mark."

Alisha knelt beside the body. "There's always a mark," she said. "You just have to look deep enough."

***

Noah stood a few feet from the tape line, close enough to see the body, far enough to pretend he hadn't seen a body before.

He had, technically. Museums preserved them. The archive had autopsy sketches from the 1800s—bad ones, drawn like maps to curses.

But this one was different.

Courbet's face wasn't just dead. It was calm.

The banyan behind him rustled, even though there was no wind.

Noah swallowed. He had always laughed at the stories as a kid—the boy in the roots, the white bird, the whispers in the cane. But that laugh had gotten quieter as he'd gotten older, especially after what happened to Mikey at university.

No one believed him about that either.

He could still see the boy in the stories, clear as folklore ever was: small hands, muddy feet, eyes wide with something between terror and devotion. No one ever drew his face right. They either made him too angelic or too demonic.

But Noah had once dreamed it. The real face.

The boy wasn't crying.

He was watching.

Just like the tree.

***

Footsteps crunched nearby—Alisha and Manu were talking low near the body. Noah blinked and straightened, adjusting his messenger bag like it might guard him from whatever memory had just slithered up his spine.

***

Later, alone in the estate's unused sitting room, Alisha stared at her reflection in the window. The room was full of expensive dust. A portrait of an unnamed colonial ancestor glared down at her.

She had returned to Île de Céleste to make peace with ghosts. Instead, she found them waiting.

She reached into her coat pocket and closed her hand around something smooth and cold.

The whistle.

She didn't remember packing it. But it was there.

Just like the case.

Waiting.

Chapter 3

The morgue in Port du Roi smelled of antiseptic and unsaid things.

Alisha stood as Dr. Clara Wei slid Jean-Michel Courbet's body into the examination bay. Mid-thirties, Chinese-Celestian, straight-backed and sharp-eyed, Clara moved with the precision of someone who trusted data more than people. Her lab coat was clean, her hair pinned immaculately, and her humour was dry enough to preserve evidence.

"No obvious trauma," she said without looking up. "Vitals collapsed fast—whatever hit him was efficient."

"Could it be natural?"

Clara gave her a sideways glance. "Don't insult both of us, Inspector."

Clara raised an eyebrow. "You know better than to ask that on your first case back."

A ghost of a smile crossed Alisha's face.

Clara leaned closer to the neck. "There. Behind the ear. Tiny puncture mark. Almost missed it."

Alisha stepped forward. "Needle?"

Clara hesitated. "More like a fang. Or a stinger."

Alisha's mind flashed to Noah's words: *'A man who dishonours the grove dies without a mark.'*

"What kind of venom kills this fast?" she asked.

"I can think of a few. Cone snail, some sea snakes. But they're hard to come by. And whoever used it knew exactly where to strike."

"So, we're not just dealing with anger. We're dealing with skill."

***

Back at the Courbet estate, the party had become a crime scene.

Manu was conducting interviews with a calmness that felt earned. His presence reminded Alisha of the banyan itself—rooted, still, and holding stories he didn't always tell.

"This is our shortlist," he said, handing her a page. "The guest list had seventy names, but only a few were close to Courbet personally. The rest were donors, developers, influencers."

Alisha scanned the names:

- Simone Courbet, wife. Calm under questioning. Possibly too calm.

- Gaspard Leroy, local real estate agent. Stood to gain from Courbet's land acquisitions.

- Anjali Dubey, cultural officer. Opposed Courbet's resort plans due to heritage concerns.

- Frère Matéo, spiritual tour guide and amateur folklorist.

"Let's start with Simone," Alisha said. "The people who act calm usually do so for a reason."

✳✳✳

Interview: Simone Courbet

She sat in her private lounge, legs crossed, expression unreadable. A perfect frame of widowhood—no tears, no trembling.

"Jean-Michel had enemies, Inspector. But they didn't kill him. The island did."

Alisha tilted her head. "The island?"

"Call it what you want. Karma. Spirits. His own guilt. He took what wasn't his. You dig up sacred places, and things start to bleed."

Alisha kept her tone neutral. "Did your husband believe that?"

Simone's gaze drifted toward the window. "Lately, yes. He hadn't slept in weeks. Kept hearing things. Kept waking up thinking someone was in the room."

"Did he mention a whistle?"

Her eyes flicked back sharply. "What did you say?"

"A whistle. Small. Silver. Shaped like a bird."

Simone hesitated. "Yes. He found one during excavation. Claimed it was old. He started carrying it everywhere."

Alisha said nothing, but inside, something shifted.

***

Alisha studied the evidence board later at the station. Beneath Courbet's photo, she pinned three words: *Banyan. Whistle. Fear.*

She heard Manu step in behind her.

"You think this was personal?"

"I think it's generational."

He nodded. "That's how things work here."

Alisha turned; eyes narrowed. "And I think someone wants us to believe this was folklore. But legends don't poison you behind the ear."

Chapter 4

The archive in Port du Roi was barely air-conditioned and smelled of old newsprint and mildew—like a place time had politely avoided. Alisha followed Noah Gopaul down narrow aisles between dusty cabinets and books stacked with more hope than order.

Noah's voice echoed slightly as he narrated.

"Most official records ignore the banyan," he said. "But in oral histories, it comes up again and again—especially in songs and funeral poems. It's always the same image: a child buried alive, a white bird flying west, and roots fed with blood."

Alisha gave him a sidelong glance. "Cheerful."

He smiled faintly. "Island history usually isn't."

They stopped at a low shelf, where he pulled out a thin binder labelled *La Plantation de l'Espérance — 1790–1795.*

"This plantation stood where Courbet's estate is now," Noah explained. "French-run. Abandoned after a fire and an epidemic. But some stories say something else happened—something unspoken."

He opened to a faded page. Scrawled in French Creole was a line that made Alisha's stomach go cold:

"Garçon là ti crié jusqu'à ki pied la mange li."

(The boy screamed until the tree ate him.)

Noah didn't speak for a long time.

His fingers rested lightly on the paper, careful not to smudge the ink even though it had long dried. He'd seen that phrase before, dozens of times, in fragments and footnotes. But it always landed the same way: like a bruise under the ribs.

He had screamed once. Not as long as the boy, maybe, but loud enough.

And no one had come.

Outside the archive, the late morning heat pressed down like a wet towel. They sat under a street awning drinking tamarind water from a vendor's cart. Alisha tapped her notebook.

"Was there ever a name for the boy?"

Noah shook his head. "Only guesses. Some say he was the child of a slave and a French mistress, others say he was a runaway who broke a taboo."

"Why kill a child?"

He looked into his cup. "To bury a secret. Or silence a witness. Or... to seal a place."

Alisha studied him for a beat. "You talk like you knew him."

Noah didn't smile this time.

"Maybe I did," he said softly. "Maybe we all do."

****

Back at the Courbet estate, Alisha and Manu walked the banyan grove again—this time deeper.

The police had cordoned off the scene, but the roots spread beyond the tape. Alisha stopped where the trees clustered into a natural archway.

"Ever hear of this boy growing up?" she asked Manu.

He shrugged. "Every child on the island hears the story, but they don't believe it. Not really. It's a bedtime warning, not a history lesson."

"Then why do so many people still leave coins in the roots?"

Manu didn't answer.

***

They turned to see Frère Matéo approaching—barefoot, dressed in white linen, with beads around his neck and a cloth bag slung over his shoulder. His beard was streaked with grey and sand.

"I know that look," he said to Alisha. "You've heard the story now. You've started listening."

Alisha studied him. "You were a guest at the party?"

"I was invited to bless the grove. Jean-Michel wanted to keep appearances." He smiled without warmth. "But he never believed. That was his mistake."

"You believe?"

Matéo knelt by the roots and placed something in them—a coin and a petal of frangipani.

"I believe the earth remembers. And some wounds don't stay buried."

He stood and turned to her; voice quiet. "Do you know about the boy in 1964?"

Alisha's breath caught. "No."

"He died here. Same spot. No killer ever found. And the autopsy said the same thing as your man: no trauma, no illness. Just... collapse."

He looked at her, something ancient in his eyes.

"You think this began with Courbet. But it didn't. It never does."

Chapter 5

The Ministry of Culture sat behind a rusted iron gate in Port du Roi's colonial quarter—a pale stone building with blue shutters and the persistent smell of jasmine and government neglect.

Inside, Anjali Dubey sat stiffly at a desk stacked with folders, petitions, and rolled maps that hadn't seen daylight in months. Her saree was crisp, her eyes sharper than her smile.

"I knew Jean-Michel Courbet would end up dead," she said, without ceremony.

Alisha blinked. "That's quite a statement."

"I didn't say I killed him. I said I knew he was courting danger."

Alisha remained standing.

"How so?"

Anjali slid a folder across the desk. Inside: a burial ledger, creased and re-copied so many times it looked more ghost than document.

"Beneath those banyans are graves. Not myths. Not whispers. Names. Coordinates. Ages."

Alisha scanned the page. Infant. Female. Unmarked. Male, age 10. Tamil-Creole.

Dates smudged, but consistent: mid-1800s to early 1900s.

Alisha looked up. "How long have you had this?"

Anjali's eyes didn't flinch. "Long enough to lose two promotions over it."

She stood and walked toward the window. Outside, vines coiled through the iron grates.

"My grandfather worked those fields. My mother used to tell me he came home with dirt in his teeth. Said the land was trying to speak through him."

She turned. "He died before I could ask what that meant."

Alisha said nothing.

"I got this job because I was the only one who remembered who he was." Anjali gave a small, bitter laugh. "And I've spent every year since trying not to forget what he might've died for."

"He wanted to build on sacred land," she continued. "Not just ancestral or spiritual—formally protected. There were burial markers beneath those banyans. Creole slave graves. Possibly Tamil indentured remains too. We tried to stop him."

"But?"

Anjali held up a stamped document. "He had this. A full reclassification permit, signed by the Tourism Minister's office, fast-tracked through legal. One week. That never happens unless someone wants it to."

Alisha took the paper, scanning the approval. "Minister Girard's signature."

Anjali nodded. "Girard and Courbet were old schoolmates. When we protested, we were told we were being 'anti-development.'"

Alisha lowered the file. "Did you protest publicly?"

"I wrote four letters. I organized a panel. I gave a speech at the university." She met Alisha's eyes. "And yes—I screamed at Courbet once, at a public forum. Told him he was digging up ghosts."

"Did you threaten him?"

"I warned him," Anjali said. "There's a difference."

"I believed in process, Inspector. I believed in facts, petitions, maps. But the bones don't care how tidy your paperwork is. They only care that they were forgotten."

She pointed toward the copy of the burial ledger. "You want to solve a murder? Start with the names they erased first."

✳✳✳

Outside, on the Ministry steps, Alisha took a deep breath. The jasmine was heavier here—sweet, cloying, and almost sickly.

Manu waited in the shade; arms crossed.

"She told you what I already told you?" he asked. "Courbet had too many friends in high places, and too little respect for what lay under his feet."

Alisha showed him the permit. "Minister Girard signed this."

Manu whistled low. "Then we've just stepped in it."

"She's passionate. Angry. But not a killer."

"No," Manu said. "But she might know who would be."

***

That afternoon, they returned to La Maison Marée. Alisha requested Courbet's private files. His estate lawyer, a thin man named Jérôme Fontaine, balked until she mentioned a court order.

They found a locked drawer in Courbet's home office.

Inside: papers detailing private land buys, payments to surveyors, and a map of the grove—marked with five red Xs.

"Graves?" Alisha murmured.

"Or something else," Manu said. "Look at this—dates next to each X."

The most recent was from a week ago.

The oldest? 1964.

***

Back at the station, Alisha stood over the whiteboard, drawing new connections.

- Courbet died under the banyan.
- *Another man* died there in 1964.
- Courbet knew. He had it on file.
- He kept digging anyway.

She underlined a new phrase:

He woke something.

***

Before the precinct could finish processing the reports from Courbet's estate, another call came in—urgent, clipped, and shaking at the edges. Jérôme Fontaine had disappeared.

Not coincidence. A pattern was forming, old as the roots beneath their feet. And the banyan was listening.

Chapter 6

The precinct was quieter than usual, but not calm. It was the kind of quiet that buzzed under the skin—the silence of a team holding its breath, unsure if they were about to speak or explode.

Alisha Desai walked past the duty desk and into the heart of the squad room, where a dozen unwritten conversations hung in the air. Manu Roux stood at the whiteboard, arms crossed, jaw tense. Clara Wei scrolled through toxin reports, her lips thin, her eyes glass-hard. Noah Gopaul paced with his ever-present notebook, mouthing something under his breath like a prayer.

She had barely sat when Manu spoke.

"Three days. Two bodies. No suspects. We look like we're chasing shadows."

"We're chasing patterns," Alisha replied.

Clara didn't look up. "You mean legends."

"Folklore carries data," Noah muttered.

"Only if you believe in bedtime stories," Clara snapped.

Noah froze mid-step. "And only if you believe *bodies* collapse naturally from rare coastal neurotoxins found in deep-sea cone snails."

The temperature in the room shifted— salt in the air, static on skin. Alisha looked between them; jaw tight.

"We need focus," she said, rising. "Let's go over what we have."

***

Manu raised a brow. "Then maybe you can share your focus, Inspector. Because we've been chasing this for three days, and all we've got is a whisper and a corpse."

The word *Inspector* hit harder than it needed to.

Alisha straightened. "I've solved harder cases with less."

"Yeah," Clara said, standing now. "Maybe where you come from, they hand you clean timelines and polite killers. But here, nothing's neutral. Not even dirt."

Noah interjected, too quickly. "She's not wrong. The land isn't just geography—it's *testimony.*"

"You know what it *is*?" Clara snapped. "Unprovable."

Alisha's voice was sharp now. "So is grief, but we don't throw that out."

Manu whistled low. "Okay. Everyone takes a breath."

They didn't.

***

As they recited the facts, Alisha watched them. Manu's voice was flat—not disengaged, just weary. Clara's hands twitched when Noah brought up folklore. And Noah—his voice cracked when he mentioned the grove by name.

Later, over lukewarm tea in the break room, the quiet was thick and personal.

Clara stared at her mug like it had betrayed her.

Alisha finally asked, softer, "You don't trust me yet."

Clara didn't blink. "You joined in the middle of a murder case. You brought new rules. You believe too quickly."

"Because I'm willing to listen?"

"Because you think that's enough."

"Do you know what it feels like," she said, setting her mug down hard, "to have years of science undermined by a story about a whispering tree?"

"Do you know what it feels like," Noah countered, "to grow up with that story and find it written in blood?"

The silence after that wasn't awkward. It was grief-shaped.

Alisha looked between them. There was no handbook for this—how to lead a team pulled in different directions by history. She thought of Raj. Of how he'd made his team feel heard, even when he didn't agree. She wasn't him. But she had to try.

Before she could speak, Zara Naik walked into the precinct like she owned it.

"Inspector," she said, holding up a file. "Thought you'd want to know who Courbet was calling the week before he died."

Alisha took it. A name stood out: Father Cassien.

Zara leaned in. "He knew your grandfather, didn't he?"

The air shifted.

Zara smirked. "The banyan's still talking, Inspector. Hope you're listening."

She left without waiting for a reply.

A junior officer knocked on the breakroom door, holding an envelope. No return address. No stamp. Just Alisha's name, scrawled in careful blue ink.

She opened it.

Inside: a piece of paper, creased down the middle. A child's drawing—crayon lines.

A large tree, gnarled and black. Five circles at its base. A silver coin in the sky. And beneath the roots, a figure with no face.

A spiral ringed by strokes curled across the corner.

Alisha didn't speak.

She turned the page over. Just one word, printed in red crayon:

"Soon."

Clara stepped back. "Is that a threat?"

Noah looked pale. "It's a ritual countdown."

Manu swore under his breath. "This isn't folklore anymore. It's performance."

Alisha stood frozen for a beat longer, then pinned the drawing to the centre of the board.

The root system was forming.

And someone was watching it grow.

They were being watched.

And tested.

By someone who knew what haunted them.

By someone who remembered.

Chapter 7

The records vault behind the Port du Roi courthouse was cold in the way old government buildings always were—as if time itself had stiffened into the stone walls and paper dust. The lights buzzed overhead, yellow and tired.

Alisha moved slowly, her fingertips skimming across fading case numbers. Noah trailed behind her, muttering citations like charms.

"You're sure it's not digitized?" she asked.

"Digitization died when the funding did," he replied. "You want ghosts? You find them in boxes."

They found the file by a handwritten label: *Belle Forêt, 1973 – UNRESOLVED.*

The folder was brittle, stuffed with mismatched paper, old photos, faded ink. Alisha opened it carefully.

There was a report of a boy's body found beneath a banyan tree. No signs of struggle. No cause of death. Locals had refused to retrieve it. The case was closed within days. On the final page: a signature.

Rajiv Desai – Inspector, 2nd District.

Alisha's breath caught. The ink of his name looked oddly fresh, though she knew it wasn't. She hadn't expected the weight of seeing it—how it twisted something low in her stomach. Her grandfather had always been a voice of control, certainty. Not someone who wrote about fear.

Noah crouched beside her, eyes scanning. He pointed to a sketch in the margins.

"That's the whistle."

A child's drawing, almost. Crude bird shape. Spiral on the wing.

"'Passed from the boy to the priest. Returned to silence,'" Noah read aloud. "Creepy."

She turned the page.

It was unlike her grandfather. Blunt. Raw. As if something had pushed past the official tone and spoken through him.

She closed her eyes for a moment. Remembered him sitting on their veranda with a cup of tea, the sound of the sea behind him. He'd never told her this. Had he wanted to?

Noah stood. "So, Courbet knew. He had to. He reached out to the same priest. Cassien. Still alive."

Alisha didn't answer. She was staring at a red stamp over the report: *SUPPRESSED*.

***

Clara stood alone in the morgue, lights dimmed, gloves off. Courbet's tox screen glowed faintly on the monitor. Still inconclusive. Still maddening.

She stared at the tiny puncture behind his ear. Barely visible. Clean. Precise. Lethal.

Clara had told herself it was just biology. Exotic venom. Perfect placement. Logical.

But it wasn't sitting right.

She reached for her notes, then stopped. Her hand was shaking.

The last time her hands shook, she was sixteen, sitting beside her grandmother as she muttered a prayer in Hakka, lighting incense for an uncle who "heard the banyan breathing" and walked into the sea.

Clara had called it madness. Called it cultural trauma.

Now the sound of rustling leaves kept slipping into her dreams.

***

Noah crouched beside Alisha, eyes on Raj's handwriting. "He believed it. So, did I. Not a spirit. Not exactly. But something that demanded to be heard."

Alisha turned the page. A note from Raj:

"I do not believe this was an act of violence as we understand it. The land has memory. I fear something was reawakened."

It felt raw, unlike anything else in the file. She closed her eyes for a moment. Thought of his quiet voice, his calm certainty. Thought of the stories he *never* told.

"I didn't know he wrote like this," she whispered.

Noah looked at her, careful. "Maybe he didn't. Maybe something wrote through him."

***

Back at the precinct, the team hovered around the copied pages. The air was thick—not just with what they read, but with what it meant.

Clara was quiet. Pale. But present.

Manu stared at Raj's note.

Alisha was already writing on the board. Five roots. Five deaths. Five sites.

"The killer isn't random," she said. "He's finishing what was buried. And Raj knew it had started decades ago."

Clara glanced at the morgue photo again. "What happens when the last root's cut?"

Alisha looked at the final line of the driftwood poem.

Both will watch the next one die.

Clara looked visibly shaken. "He wrote this in an official document? About land memory?"

"The autopsy read like mine," she added. "No trauma. Just collapse. It's repeating."

Manu was quiet for a long time.

"I remember hearing whispers about that case when I was a trainee. Nobody talked about it. Now I know why."

Noah added, "Raj Desai might have been the first root."

The phrase landed harder than Alisha expected. First root. She thought of the whistle in her drawer. How it had found her, how it felt warm sometimes without reason. As if remembering.

"We keep thinking the killer's ahead of us," she said slowly. "Maybe he's just finishing what someone else started."

They fell silent again. A low hum of traffic came in from the open window. The room felt smaller.

Then Clara said, softly, "If this keeps going, what happens when he reaches the end?"

Alisha stared at the photo of the tree in the file. The roots seemed darker than she remembered.

"Maybe that's the wrong question," she said. "Maybe we should ask what he thinks the end is for."

Manu finally spoke. "So, the priest knew Raj. And Raj knew something he never told anyone."

Alisha nodded. "Then it's time someone asks him why."

Chapter 8

Father Cassien lived in a weathered stone house near Anse Détourée, where the land sloped gently toward the cane fields and the wind always seemed to carry something old. Alisha stood at the rusted gate, the whistle in her pocket, Raj's file under her arm.

She hadn't told the team where she was going. She needed this to be hers. Not procedure. Not strategy. Just truth.

The door opened before she could knock. The old priest filled the frame, thin but upright, his eyes dark with recognition.

"You're Rajiv's granddaughter," he said.

Alisha nodded. "Inspector Desai."

He studied her for a long beat. "He had your stillness. But not your anger."

***

The sitting room smelled of sandalwood and dry paper. Books lined every surface. Icons of saints shared space with carved elephants and incense bowls. In a corner shrine, a candle flickered beside both a cross and a small brass Ganesha.

Alisha sat in silence as Father Cassien poured tea.

He moved slowly, like a man who no longer feared time.

"He spoke of you often," Cassien said.

Alisha blinked. "He did?"

"Only when he was tired. He kept his worries private. But you were the only thing that made him doubt his duty. He wanted to leave you a world worth trusting."

The whistle in her coat felt heavier.

***

Alisha slid the file onto the table. Raj's notes. His voice on the page. The spiral symbol. The whispers. The unmarked graves.

Cassien didn't touch it.

"I buried the boy myself," he said. "No one else would."

Alisha stared. "You mean the boy under the tree?"

Cassien met her eyes. "No. I mean *this* boy. The one in the file. 1973. Belle Forêt."

***

"The autopsy said natural causes."

"No trauma. No illness," Cassien said softly. "But his mouth was open. Like he died mid-story."

***

She placed the whistle between them.

Cassien flinched. Then steadied. "I thought it was lost."

Alisha: "What is it?"

"Memory," he said. "A griot's call. West African. Carried into Creole rites, Bhojpuri chants, Chinese funerals. A symbol to remember the unremembered. To summon the story that refuses to stay buried."

She ran her thumb along its wing. "Did you give it to my grandfather?"

"No. He found it." His voice softened. "And it found him."

***

She turned to the journal page. Raj's writing.

"I do not believe this was an act of violence as we understand it. The land has memory. I fear something was reawakened."

Cassien exhaled. "He stopped speaking about the case, eventually. But I knew it followed him. He used to sit under the banyan and whisper apologies to the soil."

Alisha's throat was tight. "He never told me."

"Because it wasn't over."

"He disappeared days after this report," Alisha said.

"Yes." Cassien's eyes darkened. "And not everything in that file is complete. There was a ledger he never turned in."

"Ledger?"

"Land deeds. Bribes. Name changes. He called it the *book of forgetting*. Said it showed who profited when the land stopped speaking."

Alisha's heart thudded. "Where is it?"

"I told him to hide it where no one would listen."

"Did he?"

"I don't know," Cassien said. "But the whistle came back. That means the story isn't finished."

***

Cassien said nothing more. He simply returned to his tea, watching the candle burn.

Outside, the wind shifted.

Alisha stood to leave. At the door, she paused.

"You still believe in it, don't you?"

Cassien smiled, not kindly. "Belief isn't the point, child. Memory is."

She left the shrine with more questions than answers. But one thing was clear:

She wasn't the only one searching for that ledger.

And the land?

It was still speaking.

Chapter 9

The call came just after dawn.

Alisha was already awake, sitting on her veranda with cold tea and the whistle in her palm. When the duty officer's voice crackled through the line— *"Another body. Near the heritage office."* she was already grabbing her coat.

The streets of Port du Roi were still half-asleep when she arrived. Blue lights pulsed against colonial brick and bougainvillea vines. Clara was crouched near the victim, gloved hands moving with quiet precision.

Manu met her at the cordon. "Clerk. Mid-level. Name's Rishi Sawan. Lives alone. Paperwork guy."

"How long?"

"Security cam says 4:12 a.m. Collapse. No one else on screen."

***

Rishi lay on his side near the back entrance, eyes wide, mouth slightly open. No blood. No bruises.

But something glinted on his back.

A coin—silver, aged, placed exactly at the spine's centre. Balanced like punctuation.

Clara looked up. "Same puncture mark. Behind the ear. I'll confirm, but it's the same venom profile."

Alisha closed her eyes. The third root.

***

Back at the precinct, tension spiked like fever.

Noah traced circles on the whiteboard, linking Courbet, Fontaine, Sawan. "All three were involved in land reclassification. Directly or as signatories."

"What about Anjali?", asked Manu.

Alisha said, "She tried to stop it. That might make her next."

Noah pulled up a scanned page from the file Cassien mentioned—an old land transfer form. The signature at the bottom? Rishi Sawan.

"Courbet's land. Fontaine's estate. Charamond Plantation. All passed through his desk."

Clara crossed her arms. "So, he wasn't just a clerk. He was the architect of forgetting."

Alisha turned to the board. "Three down. Two to go. It's not random. It's a ritual ledger."

Manu swore softly. "That land's never been touched. They tried to build a guesthouse there in the 90s. It burned before it opened."

Alisha said nothing. She was already thinking ahead.

***

Clara leaned against the desk. She hadn't sat down since the scene. She kept re-checking the tox report, though she already knew what it would say.

"Three bodies," she said. "No noise. No struggle. It's like they *agree* to die."

"Maybe they do. Some guilt's too old to speak," said Noah.

Clara didn't respond.

***

The site came into view like a wound reopened.

The Charamond site was quiet, swallowed by cane and creeping vines. No police tape. No footprints. Just wind and rustling leaves.

They found the marker by accident—a moss-covered stone barely visible at the foot of an overgrown archway. Beneath it, the soil had been disturbed.

Noah knelt. "Someone dug here. Recently. Then resealed it. Badly."

Clara brushed aside leaves. "This was a grave."

Manu stepped back. "So, what did he take?"

Alisha stared at the uneven dirt. "Not what. Who."

No one spoke for a moment.

Then Noah whispered, "Bastian."

***

Back at the station, the precinct buzzed like a disturbed hive. Officers muttered about omens. Someone found a crow feather on the squad room windowsill. Superstition crept in, no matter how often Clara rolled her eyes.

Alisha stood before the whiteboard; arms crossed.

"Three down. Two to go. And every step is mapped."

She looked at the poem again.

One saw truth, one sang lies.

Her voice was quiet.

"If Raj was the one who saw truth... Sawan was the one who sang lies. He made the land forget."

Clara, still shaken, asked, "What happens when the killer finishes the poem?"

Alisha looked at the final line.

Both will watch the next one die.

She didn't answer.

Because the next root was already chosen.

***

A junior officer entered. "Ma'am. This came in the precinct Dropbox."

Another envelope. No markings. No return. Just the weight of something unfinished.

Inside was a pressed leaf—banyan—dried and veined with red ink. Ink shaped like a spiral.

On the back was a line in careful handwriting.

"The ledger has five names. The land remembers all of them."

Alisha's spine prickled.

The root system was still growing.

****

Somewhere on Île de Céleste the killer was reflecting on the ledger:

Five names.

Five roots.

Five coins paid.

The land was never quiet.

They only taught us to stop listening.

I learned to hear again. In the spaces between breaths. In the silence that follows memory.

The banyan groans when it's hungry.

Courbet gave me his arrogance. Fontaine gave me his lies. Sawan gave me his silence.

The girl will give me her defiance.

The last one—he will give me his history.

I don't do this for punishment. Or revenge.

I do it for restoration.

The land remembers. I only write it down.

Chapter 10

Rain threaded the sky like silver stitches as Alisha stared out the precinct window. The banyan leaf was still on her desk; red spiral dried to a dark scab. She hadn't touched it since the envelope arrived.

Behind her, the room hummed with quiet friction. Everyone was moving, but no one was moving *together*.

***

Noah leaned in the doorway, arms crossed, voice low.

"You ever think about the ones who believed before you did?" he asked.

Alisha didn't turn around. "All the time."

He stepped closer. Sat without asking.

"His name was Mikey. Student assistant. Back when I was documenting oral stories in Lavande. He thought that everything we recorded was *real*. Started drawing the symbols before we even translated them."

"I told him to chill. To stop obsessing. Told him stories didn't kill people."

He paused.

"Until they did."

Alisha finally looked at him.

"He went missing during a storm. Found two days later, face-up in a field. No marks. Just... gone inside. Like someone took the part of him that listened and burned it out."

"He drew a tree. Same spiral. Same coin. But the bird? It had no eyes. No mouth."

Noah shook his head. "I never published the interview that led us there. Buried it. Because I didn't want to admit he might've been right."

"Now I dream in roots. So yeah. I believe."

***

Back in the squad room, Clara slammed a folder shut.

"You brought in Father Cassien without protocol. We can't afford to look like we're chasing ghost stories while someone's leaving bodies in alleyways."

Alisha didn't flinch. "He buried the first boy. He knew Raj."

"And that makes him trustworthy?" Clara snapped. "You're chasing your grandfather's shadow, not a suspect."

"She's not wrong. Raj's report was suppressed. That ledger still matters," Noah said.

Manu raised a brow. "And if it leads to someone untouchable?"

"Then we touch them anyway," Alisha said.

****

A junior officer arrived with a surveillance still: Anjali Dubey arguing with Sawan the day before he died. Her hand on his arm. His face tight. No audio.

"You think she knew?" Clara asked.

"You think she helped?" Manu added, quieter.

Alisha stared at the image. She wanted to say no. That Anjali was too broken by the system to break it in return.

But that's the thing about grief. It can burn righteous. Or it can turn sharp and surgical.

***

The road to Charamond twisted inland through tall cane fields and cracked asphalt, the air thick with the scent of earth and rotting fruit. Alisha drove in silence. Noah sat beside her, rereading the poem for the hundredth time. Manu and Clara followed in the second vehicle, both quiet.

The site came into view like a wound reopened.

Charamond Plantation had once belonged to a wealthy Creole family, long abandoned after the main house burned. A half-collapsed fountain choked with weeds marked the centre, and the sugar fields—unworked for decades—had turned wild.

The wind stirred as they stepped out.

Noah moved toward a sagging stone archway. "The ledger had five sites. This was the fourth."

They spread out. Alisha moved slowly, eyes on the ground. She stopped near a cluster of wild banana trees, where the soil was darker, looser.

She knelt.

The grave was shallow, recently filled. A flat stone had been laid on top, carved with three shapes: a bird, a wave, and the now-familiar spiral ringed by five strokes.

Clara crouched beside her. "This was deliberate. Whoever dug here knew what they were looking for."

"Or what they were returning," Noah murmured.

Manu stood back; arms crossed. "If we didn't know better, I'd say he's following a ritual."

Alisha traced the spiral with one gloved hand. The stone was cool. "He's marking them. One by one."

Clara glanced up. "But what for?"

Alisha didn't answer. Her eyes stayed on the stone. It didn't feel like a grave. It felt like a countdown.

***

Back at the precinct, the atmosphere was brittle. Everyone felt it. One wrong breath would snap the air.

Alisha gathered the team in the briefing room. The whiteboard was now a storm of threads, maps, and photos.

"He's not choosing people randomly," she said. "They're all tied to the land reclassification. Everyone."

"Except Raj," Noah added. "He wasn't complicit. He tried to stop it."

"And that made him the first root," Manu said grimly.

Clara sat with her arms crossed. She hadn't spoken much since Charamond. Finally, she said, "If this is some cleansing ritual, what happens to the last person? What's left when it's complete?"

"Memory," Noah said quietly. "That's what the whistle was for."

The words hung in the room like smoke.

***

That night, alone in her flat, Alisha pulled the whistle from the drawer. She stared at it. Didn't blow it.

Just held it.

The spiral on the coin. The spiral on the leaf. The spiral on Mikey's sketch. On Bastian's gravestone.

What if the killer wasn't just copying the story?

What if they were *finishing* it?

Chapter 11

Interrogation Room 2. Windowless. Fluorescent buzz. No mirror. Just silence, four walls, and a woman who's been betrayed one too many times.

****

Anjali Dubey sat with her arms crossed, jaw tight. Her hair was tied back with surgical precision. The kind of woman who never let emotion slip—until someone made it spill.

Across the table, Alisha laid down the surveillance still. Sawan. Anjali. That flash of tension in grayscale.

"You argued with him the day before he died."

"I argued with *everyone* in that department," Anjali said. "If that made me dangerous, half the Ministry would be buried under your banyan."

Noah leaned against the wall, quiet. Manu sat beside Alisha, watching Anjali like a cracked clock—waiting for the tick.

***

Alisha didn't pull out files. She pulled out the whistle.

She placed it on the table. Said nothing.

Anjali blinked.

"Where did you get that?"

"Raj Desai kept it. My grandfather," Alisha said. "He tried to stop what was coming. You knew him."

Anjali's hands didn't move. But her voice lost its edge.

"He was the only one who listened to the land and didn't ask for a grant afterward."

A long pause.

"Did he ever tell you what he saw?" Anjali asked.

Alisha: "No."

"Then you're lucky."

***

Anjali leaned forward, slowly, like something was peeling inside her.

"It was 1999. A survey team found an old burial pit under Charamond. Six skeletons. One was a child."

"They didn't report it. I was told to falsify the grid data. Bury it again."

Clara flinched from behind the glass.

"That night, I stayed late. I was angry. I went back alone."

"I heard wind. Except... nothing was moving. No trees. No frogs. Just the sound of breath. Under the dirt."

Her voice shook.

"I heard a voice. A child's voice. He said: '*It hurts to be forgotten.*'"

***

Alisha asked softly, "Why didn't you tell anyone?"

Anjali sighed, "Because I thought I imagined it. Until Raj came. And he said, 'If the roots scream, don't listen too long. You'll go with them.'"

"He gave me a page from the ledger. Said to keep it away from the Ministry. I burned it six years ago. But the spiral still shows up. On documents. In my dreams."

She laughed, short and bitter.

"You want to know if I killed Sawan? No. But I wanted him dead. That make me guilty enough?"

***

"The land doesn't forget," she whispered.

"It just waits for someone who will."

***

Twelve years ago

Raj Desai stood alone under the banyan behind the Ministry at twilight. Rain was on the edge of falling.

He held the whistle in his palm.

It was lighter than it should've been. And yet it pulled at him—like it was made of everything he never said out loud.

The boy was already dead. Found beneath the banyan. No wounds. No noise. Just gone.

Raj had written it up. Called it unexplained cardiac arrest. Internally, he'd written a second version. The one that never made it into the file.

The one that started with:

"There was a voice in the soil."

He stood at the edge of the roots, coat damp, shoes muddy. He wasn't a spiritual man. But he wasn't blind, either.

"I know you're listening," he said softly. "I don't know what we woke. But it was never sleeping."

He crouched, placed the whistle near the roots.

"I'm sorry I wrote you down. Sorry I tried to explain you. You don't want to be named. You want to be remembered."

The tree did not move. But it *breathed.*

He could feel it through his knees. A pressure. A hum. Not sound—*memory*.

Raj straightened. Wiped his hands. Looked up toward the old lights flickering along the Ministry roofline.

"I'll keep the ledger," he whispered. "But not forever. Someday, someone will have to finish this story."

Then he walked back toward the building. Away from the tree.

The whistle stayed behind, half-buried in wet leaves. Waiting.

Chapter 12

It started with a smell.

Not blood. Not rot.

Incense.

Sweet. Old. Familiar in the way memories are familiar. Like something from a shrine your grandmother never let you touch.

***

The body was found near the old Chinese cemetery at Grand Rivière. Half in the shade of a bodhi tree. Laid out like a ceremony.

It was Manan Dass, a local developer and silent investor in Courbet's cultural resort scheme.

Alisha stood just beyond the perimeter, rain prickling her coat. The team moved in quiet sync behind her. But something about this scene was... different.

Clara crouched beside the body. "Same puncture mark. But something's changed."

"He was *posed*," she added. "Look at the hands."

They were placed over his chest. Palms up. A coin in one. A slip of cloth in the other.

*****

Noah stepped closer, eyes narrowing.

"That's joss paper," he said. "Burned offerings. Hakka funerary rite."

"The killer's *blending rituals*," Manu muttered. "Why?"

Alisha didn't answer. Her gaze had caught on something else.

Carved into the bark behind the body:

a full spiral, completed. A second one beside it, unfinished.

"One left," she said. "And he knows we know it."

*****

As they bagged the evidence, Clara paused—staring at Manan's face.

"He looks calm," she said.

Alisha nodded slowly. "So did Bastian. And Fontaine. And Sawan. Even Courbet. Like they weren't surprised."

Noah said, "Maybe they weren't."

***

When they returned at the precinct, there was a folder on Alisha's desk. No note. No fingerprints.

Inside was a single page from the ledger. Yellowed. Smudged. One name redacted in ink.

At the bottom:

"When the fifth root falls, the land will speak again."

She looked at the redacted name. The ink glistened like blood.

"He's holding the final name. And he wants us to find it too late."

***

That night, Clara returned to the morgue.

She wasn't supposed to. No new body. No analysis pending.

But she stood before Manan's corpse and whispered:

"What did you hear before it happened?"

No answer, of course.

But the smell of incense lingered.

And when she turned around...

...a spiral was drawn in condensation on the inside of the morgue window.

Chapter 13

The minister's office was all glass and teak and the faint scent of controlled climate. Alisha stood across from Alain Girard, watching him carefully. His smile was diplomatic, polished, but not warm.

"You understand, Inspector," he said, "this level of political sensitivity makes it very easy to misread paperwork."

"You approved three reclassification requests," Alisha replied. "All of which led to a body."

Girard's eyes didn't flinch. "My office facilitates economic growth. We don't vet folklore."

"You vetted silence. That's more dangerous."

He folded his hands. "You're here because you want someone to blame. But sometimes, ghosts haunt themselves. Let's not chase shadows when you have facts to follow."

Alisha stared at him a moment longer. Then left.

***

Anjali had just made tea. Jasmine. Too much sugar. Always did.

She sat at her desk, rereading Raj's journal page for the twelfth time.

"If you forget the boy, the roots remember."

The whistle lay beside her. Older than memory. She had meant to give it to Alisha, but something in her hesitated.

Not yet. Not tonight.

She stood to close the window. The wind had picked up. But the air was wrong—too still to stir leaves, too thick with silence. The frogs had stopped. Again.

A sound behind her. Not a footstep. Not breath.

The absence of sound.

Anjali turned.

Her mouth opened. No scream came.

The wind whispered something she did not understand.

Then, silence.

***

When Alisha returned to the precinct, dusk was falling. The squad room lights were low, and the team was scattered. Manu paced near the window, Clara scribbled notes at her lab station, and Noah sat with a vacant expression, a book of funeral rites open on his lap.

No one said much.

Then an officer called out from the entryway.

"There's something on the gate."

They moved as one.

A figure hung from the metal gate. Carved from driftwood, shaped like a child. The mouth was stitched shut with red thread. Embedded in the chest: a silver coin.

Around the figure's neck, a string of tiny beads—Creole mourning tokens.

Pinned beneath it was another poem.

Five roots buried; five coins paid

Three have fallen, two delayed

One saw truth, one sang lies

Both will watch the next one die

"This isn't escalation," Noah said. "It's an invitation."

Clara whispered, "It's not about fear. It's about control."

Manu was stone-faced. "It's a threat. But it's also a message. He's telling us he knows what's next."

Alisha didn't speak. She stared at the stitched mouth, the coin, the poem. Then she turned and walked back inside.

In the briefing room, the team gathered around the whiteboard again. No one touched the tea. No one sat.

Alisha looked at each of them. "He's not just killing. He's curating memory. Turning the island into a stage."

She paused, then pointed to the map.

"Four sites marked. One left. Whoever the next root is, he's already chosen them."

"Then we find them," Manu said.

Noah circled a name. "Anjali Dubey. She's the last surviving person who publicly opposed Courbet. And her signature doesn't appear on any waiver."

"She tried to stop it," Clara said.

"Which means," Alisha finished, "she may already be missing."

***

They arrived at Anjali's apartment just past nine. No answer. The lights were on. The door was locked from the inside.

They forced it.

Inside: a half-drunk cup of tea. An open laptop. Shoes neatly lined by the door. No sign of struggle. But on the desk—

A whistle. Cracked. Older than the one Alisha carried.

And beside it, folded neatly, a page torn from Raj Desai's journal.

Underlined in red:

If you forget the boy, the roots remember.

Chapter 14

The apartment was a quiet scream.

Alisha moved through it slowly, her flashlight playing across bookshelves, open files, handwritten notes. The whistle on the desk looked brittle, as if it had aged a hundred years in one night. Its surface was darker now—blackened, like it had been burned from the inside out.

The journal page was unmistakably Raj's. His handwriting curved with familiar restraint, underlined twice in red:

If you forget the boy, the roots remember.

"She didn't run," Manu said. "She followed the story."

Clara pointed to the window. "No signs of forced entry. Whoever it was, she let them in."

Noah stood silent in the doorway. He hadn't touched anything. He hadn't spoken since they arrived. Finally, he said, "This is a reenactment. A restoration. They're being taken in the order the land was erased."

Alisha's pulse throbbed.

Five roots. Five sites. Each death a ritual.

Courbet. Sawan. Fontaine. The unmarked grave. Now Anjali.

Or maybe not yet.

"We don't know how long she's been gone," Clara said, checking her watch. "No blood. No struggle. She could still be alive."

Alisha nodded. "Then we find her. No breakaways. No heroes. We end this as a team."

***

The board now resembled a shrine—veins of red string stretching across names, sites, and poems.

A pressed black petal had appeared, pinned without explanation to the precinct bulletin board. Nobody admitted placing it. Nobody dared remove it.

"He's recreating the ledger," Noah said, tracing the strings. "Each site, each act—mapped to memory. Four completed. One left."

Chapter 15

The precinct was silent, but no one was still.

They'd decoded the ledger. Five names. Five deaths. Each tied to reclassified land—except one.

"There's a gap," Noah said. "One site has no paperwork. Hidden—even from the ledger."

Clara looked up.

"Alisha. Your family home sits on exempted land. Technically unclaimed. You weren't just following the spiral... you were born into it."

Alisha stared at the board.

"So, the final root... is me."

A knock interrupted.

A junior officer burst in. "Ma'am. Anjali Dubey. GPS ping from her watch—chapel ruins, Belle Forêt sector. Signal just died."

Alisha's voice was low. "That's where Raj went before they silenced his report."

Noah added, "If the murderer is finishing the ritual, that's where it ends. Not your house—your bloodline's origin."

"Raj's last note mentioned a chapel," Manu added. "North of Belle Forêt. His final case before he vanished."

Alisha pulled up a satellite image. Overgrown ruins. No records. No development. "That's it. It's the last place not touched by reclassification."

Clara scanned the room. "If he's finishing the ritual, he'll do it there."

"And if Anjali's alive," Alisha said, "that's where he's holding her."

Noah swallowed. "So, what's the fifth act meant to be?"

Alisha stared at the spiral map.

"Completion," she said. "And remembrance."

"We go now," Alisha said.

***

The precinct lights flickered as an envelope appeared on Alisha's desk—no seal, no stamp.

Inside was a pressed black petal and a note:

The land does not forgive.

It blooms what it buries.

Come home.

Clara frowned. "He's baiting you."

Alisha nodded.

"He wants me to go to the wrong place.
But I know where it ends."

Chapter 16

They arrived just before dawn. The sky was ash-grey, the mist thick with dew and something heavier. The kind of air that remembered screams.

Manu checked his gear. "Quiet entry. No splits. No noise."

Alisha nodded. "We finish this together."

The chapel had once been stone and hymns. Now it was skeletal—pews broken, altar collapsed. Beneath the pulpit, a faint glow flickered.

A cellar.

Alisha descended first. The wood groaned like a throat.

They found Anjali seated on a stone. Wrists bound, yes—but she wasn't afraid. She looked up, eyes burning.

"Took you long enough," she whispered hoarsely.

She shifted slightly, revealing symbols etched into the stone around her: a bird, a spiral, five roots.

From the shadow behind her, the killer emerged.

Danyel Maurel.

Slim. Clean. Early 30s. His face wasn't cruel—it was calm. Almost devout.

He raised his hands. No struggle. No protest.

"I've done what I came to do," he said.

***

Alisha stepped forward, her voice flint.

"Which was what? A string of murders?"

"To remember," Danyel said softly. "For the land. For the boy. For the names removed by silence."

"You killed people."

"I made them symbols. Every one of them helped bury something sacred. I helped it speak."

"And Raj?" Her voice cracked. "My grandfather?"

"He was the first to understand. They silenced him. I continued his work."

The room held its breath.

Manu moved to cuff him. Clara checked Anjali. Noah walked the edge of the cellar, eyes on the wall.

There, scorched into stone:

"If the boy is forgotten, the land will scream until someone listens."

Alisha stared at Danyel.

"You think this is justice? This is just more blood."

"No," he said quietly. "This is memory. Memory needs a voice."

He looked to the spiral burning behind him—not a symbol now, but a presence. A watcher.

"The roots are listening."

Chapter 17

Danyel Maurel sat in the interview room with his wrists cuffed and his spine straight. He didn't blink much. Didn't fidget. He stared at the mirror like he could see through it, like the people watching were part of his audience.

Alisha watched him through the glass. Behind her, Manu and Clara stood silent. Noah had stepped out for air.

"He's too calm," Clara said. "Like he rehearsed this."

"He did," Manu replied. "We just didn't read the script until it was too late."

Alisha stepped into the room alone.

Danyel turned to her and smiled faintly. "Inspector Desai."

She sat. Placed the whistle on the table. "Why them?"

"Because they were written into the earth wrong." He didn't hesitate. "Their names buried other names. Real ones. Sacred ones. Land is memory, Inspector. And they built their futures on stolen bones."

"And what about your future?" she asked.

"Mine?" He tilted his head. "I was just the reader. The story was already there."

Alisha opened a folder. Photos of the sites. The ledger. Courbet. Sawan. Fontaine. "So, you thought if you killed enough of them, someone would remember the boy?"

"Not remember," Danyel said. "*Listen.* Memory without listening is just a museum."

She leaned in slightly. "You planned this for years."

He nodded. "It began with Raj. He left gaps I couldn't ignore. Footnotes in court logs, entries in cancelled land claims. A ledger buried with meaning. They thought they could silence a man like that. But the island kept speaking. I just gave it language."

Alisha folded her arms. "You called murder language."

"Symbols," he corrected. "Sacrifice. The ones who died were never innocent. Some held the pen. Others just closed the book."

She stared at him for a moment. "And Anjali?"

His voice dropped. "She was the final witness. Not a death. A reckoning."

Outside the glass, Manu whispered, "He was going to let her go. After the ritual."

Clara shook her head. "No. He wanted her to tell the story. Like a priestess."

***

[Flashback – After Danyel's Arrest]

Among Danyel's belongings, Noah found a folded drawing tucked inside a hand-stitched journal. The ink was faded but precise—a crude map of five marked locations. Four were already labelled with initials. The fifth: *F.*

Next to it, scrawled in the corner, a phrase in Bhojpuri:

"Justice returns to the root that signed in silence."

Alisha and Manu exchanged a look.

"Fontaine," she said.

The estate on Rue Charamond was gated and silent. Lights on timers. No visible movement.

They broke through the side entrance and found him in the study—slumped, mouth ajar, breathing shallow.

Clara checked his pulse. "He's alive. Same toxin. Just enough to paralyze."

Pinned to his lapel: a silver coin.

Alisha stood still for a long time.

"Fontaine drafted the 1964 Espérance land transfer," she said. "He didn't just enable it. He codified it. The ritual ends with the one who made it legal."

***

Later that night, Alisha returned to her office. The precinct was quiet. The kind of quiet that came after storms.

The ledger sat on her desk. So did the whistle.

She looked at the board one last time. Five sites. Five stories. A ritual finished.

Or just begun.

Her team had done their part. Clara was back in the lab, rebuilding trust in her tools. Manu had finally stopped calling the case a curse. Noah had sent her an old song—something Bhojpuri about a bird that sings only once before it dies.

She turned back to the ledger.

Raj's handwriting was there. So was a name she hadn't noticed before.

Bastian.

Underlined. Circled.

A name the land hadn't let go.

Chapter 18

The case file was thin.

Not because there wasn't enough evidence. But because some truths don't fit inside paperwork.

Danyel Maurel had confessed without hesitation. Named every site, every root. Said the words not like a killer—but like a keeper of stories.

He didn't ask for a lawyer.

He asked for a tree to be planted at each grave.

***

Case File Summary – Inspector Alisha Desai

Subject: Danyel Maurel

Charges: Premeditated murders. Ritual homicides. Suppression of state records.

Status: In custody. No legal defence entered.

Recovered Statements:

"I didn't kill them. I remembered them. The coin only matters if someone forgets."

He confessed with reverence. Not guilt.

***

The press conference was scheduled for noon. The room at the Ministry of Justice buzzed with low voices, camera clicks, and the sound of politeness stretched to breaking.

Alisha stood behind the podium, her notes folded once in her hand, unread. She had barely slept. The whistle rested in her coat pocket, a weight that had become too familiar to forget. The ledger—Raj's truth— sat in the Ministry's vault. But it wasn't the ledger she feared.

It was the faces.

The ministers. The reporters. The people watching at home.

She could feel her team behind her. Manu, a wall of presence. Clara, outwardly composed but blinking too fast. Noah, turning something small over in his hand— a charm his grandmother had once tied to his satchel for luck.

They were with her. But they were scared too.

What if the island turned against them?

What if exposing the truth meant burning the peace?

She cleared her throat.

"The investigation into the recent deaths tied to historical land transfers has concluded with the arrest of Danyel Maurel," she began. Her voice did not tremble. "A man driven not by madness, but by a belief that the island had unfinished stories to tell. Stories that were buried under wealth, silence, and bureaucracy."

Cameras flashed.

"The victims were not random. They were participants in a long arc of erasure. Their deaths were not justified. But neither were the lives they lived untouched by consequence."

She paused. Her throat was dry. Her hands were still.

"The ledger kept by Rajiv Desai—my grandfather—will be submitted for independent tribunal review. I will not be the one to decide which names are remembered and which are forgotten. But I will ensure they are all heard."

More flashes. A quiet buzz of journalists exchanging glances.

She stepped back.

Manu gave her a quiet nod. Clara exhaled through her nose. Noah smiled, barely.

They had stepped into history. Together.

****

That evening, in the squad room, the team sat around the briefing table with mugs of lukewarm tea. The board had been wiped clean. For the first time in weeks, there were no threads. No photos. Just four people, tired and thoughtful.

"We did the right thing," Clara said.

"We did the hard thing," Noah replied.

Manu added, "And we didn't lose each other in the process. That counts for something."

Alisha didn't speak for a while. Her shoulders were tense. Her eyes on the wall.

"I kept wondering today if someone would throw a stone," she said quietly. "If we were pulling a thread that the island couldn't afford to lose."

She looked down at the whistle in her palm.

"I used to think justice was something you could finish," she said. "Like a case file."

She set the whistle down.

"But now I think it's a song. And someone always has to carry the next verse."

Outside, the wind shifted.

***

Manu took two weeks off. Said nothing. Just vanished into the hills.

Clara filed her report with scientific precision, then threw out every old tox report she'd kept in her drawer.

Noah returned to the university. But instead of lectures, he began building an archive—oral histories only. No redactions. No corrections. Just memory.

***

Alisha stood beneath the banyan one last time.

No badge. No uniform. Just the whistle.

She placed it at the base of the roots, where the soil still remembered her grandfather's steps.

"You wanted someone to finish the story," she said aloud.

"But I'm not the ending. I'm the echo."

The wind stirred. The leaves rustled— not loud, not fierce.

Just... present.

Epilogue

A year passed.

The tribunal held its hearings. Some names were read aloud. Others were redacted. Protests flickered, then faded. A few statues came down. A handful of street names changed. New plaques appeared where none had been allowed before.

But the banyan grove stood the same.

Alisha visited it on the anniversary of Courbet's death. She brought no flowers, no offerings. Just a breath held in the hush between winds. She stood with her hands in her pockets, the whistle resting quietly in her coat lining.

Behind her, the island moved on—slowly. No longer pretending not to remember. Not always willing to face what it did.

She didn't stay long.

***

Somewhere in the shade of the banyan, a child's voice whispered:

"It doesn't hurt anymore."

***

Pinned to the back of the file Alisha submitted to archives:

A single line, written in Raj Desai's hand.

***

In the precinct, a new case was waiting. Something strange—a broken lantern found floating in the harbour, filled with old bone and twine.

Clara frowned. Noah muttered something about a sailor's myth. Manu just raised a brow.

Alisha looked at the object for a long time. Then picked it up.

Outside, the wind moved through the banyan leaves.

Not an ending. Not anymore.